Dear Parents and Educators,

Welcome to Penguin Young Readers! As parents and educators, you know that each child develops at his or her own pace—in terms of speech, critical thinking, and, of course, reading. Penguin Young Readers recognizes this fact. As a result, each Penguin Young Readers book is assigned a traditional easy-to-read level (1–4) as well as a Guided Reading Level (A–P). Both of these systems will help you choose the right book for your child. Please refer to the back of each book for specific leveling information. Penguin Young Readers features esteemed authors and illustrators, stories about favorite characters, fascinating nonfiction, and more!

Peanut Butter's First Day of School

LEVEL **2**

GUIDED READING LEVEL **I**

This book is perfect for a **Progressing Reader** who:
- can figure out unknown words by using picture and context clues;
- can recognize beginning, middle, and ending sounds;
- can make and confirm predictions about what will happen in the text; and
- can distinguish between fiction and nonfiction.

Here are some **activities** you can do during and after reading this book:
- Make Connections: Peanut Butter was scared for his first day of school. His friends gave him advice about how to get ready. What do you do to get ready for school?
- Make Predictions: At the end of the story, Peanut Butter has finished his first day of school. He then walks home with his friends. How do you think his second day of school will be?

Remember, sharing the love of reading with a child is the best gift you can give!

—Sarah Fabiny, Editorial Director
  Penguin Young Readers program

*Penguin Young Readers are leveled by independent reviewers applying the standards developed by Irene Fountas and Gay Su Pinnell in *Matching Books to Readers: Using Leveled Books in Guided Reading*, Heinemann, 1999.

PENGUIN YOUNG READERS
An Imprint of Penguin Random House LLC

Library of Congress Cataloging-in-Publication Data is available.

ISBN 9781524784843 (pbk)   10 9 8 7 6 5 4 3 2 1
ISBN 9781524784850 (hc)   10 9 8 7 6 5 4 3 2 1

PEANUT BUTTER'S
FIRST DAY OF SCHOOL

by Terry Border

Penguin Young Readers
An Imprint of Penguin Random House

Peanut Butter was scared.

Tomorrow was the first day

of school!

Peanut Butter was new in town,

but he had already made some

friends.

"You should practice your walk to school," Mom said.

Peanut Butter thought that was a good idea.

On his walk, Peanut Butter ran
into Cupcake.

"Cupcake, what should I do to get
ready for school tomorrow?"
he asked.

"You should wear some
new sprinkles," she said.
"It's so much fun getting frosted
and sprinkled!"
Peanut Butter thanked Cupcake,
but he didn't have any sprinkles.

Peanut Butter kept walking

until he saw Egg.

"Egg, what should I do to get

ready for school tomorrow?"

he asked.

"Why don't you tell a joke?"

Egg said.

"Your jokes always crack me up."

Peanut Butter thanked Egg,

but he couldn't think of any jokes.

Peanut Butter saw Soup

in the park.

"Soup, do you have any ideas

for how I should get ready for

school tomorrow?" he asked.

Soup held out his spoon.

It had two letters,

an "N" and an "O."

"Thanks anyway,"

Peanut Butter said.

Peanut Butter sat on the bench.

He was worried about school.

None of his friends

could help at all!

Just then, Jelly ran over.

"Hey, Peanut Butter," she said.

"Do you want to join

our soccer game?"

Peanut Butter was worried about

school, but soccer would be fun.

Peanut Butter played soccer
with his friends.

He had a lot of fun.

At the end of the game,

Jelly gave Peanut Butter a hug.

"I can't wait for school," she said.

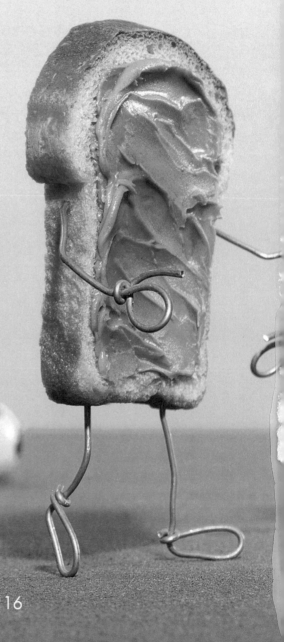

Peanut Butter did not say
anything.

He was still scared.

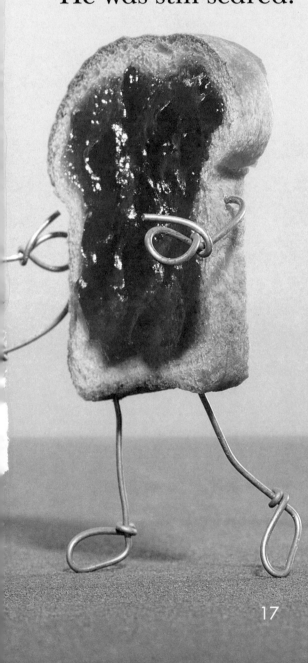

Peanut Butter walked home.

He did not have any sprinkles

to wear.

He did not have any jokes to tell.

He did not want to go to school.

The next day,

Peanut Butter walked to school.

When he got to school,

he saw Cupcake in the hallway.

"I like your sprinkles," he said.

"Thank you," Cupcake said.

"Let's walk to class together."

Peanut Butter did not know

everyone in class.

"Sit next to me," Egg said.

"I want you to meet Apple."

"Hi," Apple said.

At recess, Peanut Butter could not

find his friends.

"You must be new,"

Ice Cream said.

"You should play with us."

Peanut Butter had fun at recess.

After recess, Peanut Butter

learned a lot of new words.

sweet
sour
spicy

He even visited the library and

picked out a new book to read.

When school was over,

Peanut Butter ran over

and gave Jelly a hug.

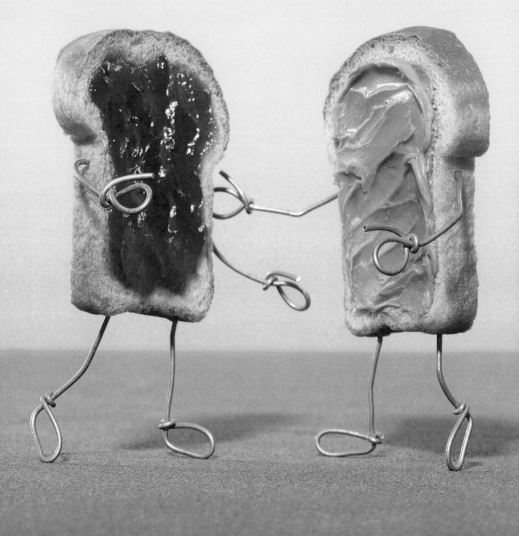

"How was your first day?"

Jelly asked.

"It was okay," Peanut Butter said.

"I made a lot of new friends.

I learned a lot of new words.

I picked out a new book to read."

"Let's walk home as a group,"
Apple said.

"We can all go together," Jelly said.

"Just like Peanut Butter and Jelly!"
Cupcake said.